HELLO from Five Time Zones

Dear Reader

Whenever I travel to countries around the world, I'm always interested by the time changes between each country in each time zone.

"TRAVEL" TO FIVE TIME ZONES TO SEE HOW KIDS AROUND THE WORLD LIVE!

I thought it would be interesting to write this book using emails – as if five kids from five different time zones wrote them to you about their city.

Better still, they have to convince you that their city is the best one in the world to live in. Think about what you would write about the place you live in, if you had to write an email for this book.

I hope you enjoy reading the kids' emails!

Sharon Parsons

For learning solutions, visit cengage.com.au

Contents

HELLO
from Five Time Zones

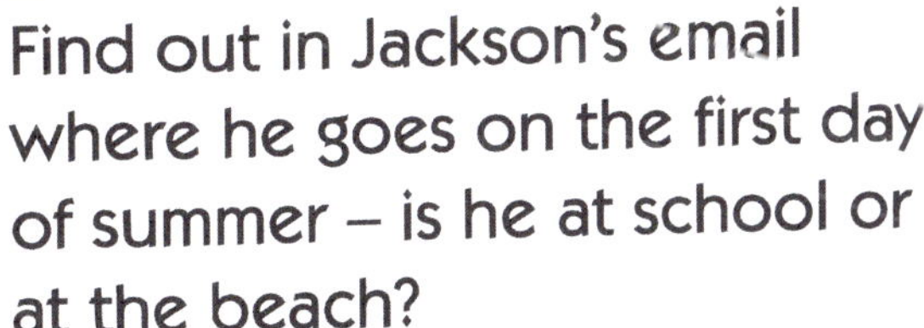

1 A Time-Zone Competition

Time for Emails

In the Time-Zone Competition you will learn about five cities in five different time zones:

- Vancouver, Canada
- London, UK
- Moscow, Russia
- Singapore, Republic of Singapore
- Melbourne, Australia.

Five Students in Five Time Zones

Five imaginary students aged nine years old have written emails at the same time in five different time zones.

Competition Rules

Each student's task is to convince you that their city is the best in the world. They will tell you the reasons why their city is the best to visit on 1 December. They will use these headings:

- place
- time
- date
- day
- season
- weather
- climate
- air quality
- environment
- city highlights.

You're the Judge

Your task is to be the judge. This is what you do:

- read each student's email
- write a score on a separate piece of paper for each part of their email
- add up all the scores for each student.

Physical Science

Seasons in Australia and New Zealand

Different countries start their seasons on different dates. In Australia and New Zealand, their Southern Hemisphere seasons start on:

1 December: summer (almost winter in the Northern Hemisphere)
1 March: autumn (almost spring in the Northern Hemisphere)
1 June: winter (almost summer in the Northern Hemisphere)
1 September: spring (almost autumn in the Northern Hemisphere)

24 Time Zones of the World

Earth is divided into 24 time zones. Each time zone is one hour apart. Countries base their times on these 24 time zones. In Australia, there are three time zones:

- eastern (New South Wales, Victoria, Queensland, Tasmania, Australian Capital Territory)
- central (South Australia, Northern Territory, Broken Hill NSW)
- western (Western Australia).

Universal Coordinated Time (UTC)

Universal Coordinated Time (UTC) is the time zone that is used to work out times in all other time zones around the world. London is in the UTC time zone. On this map, it is 12 o'clock in the morning in London. It is one o'clock in the morning in the next time zone to the east (add one hour). It is 11 o'clock at night in the next time zone to the west (subtract one hour).

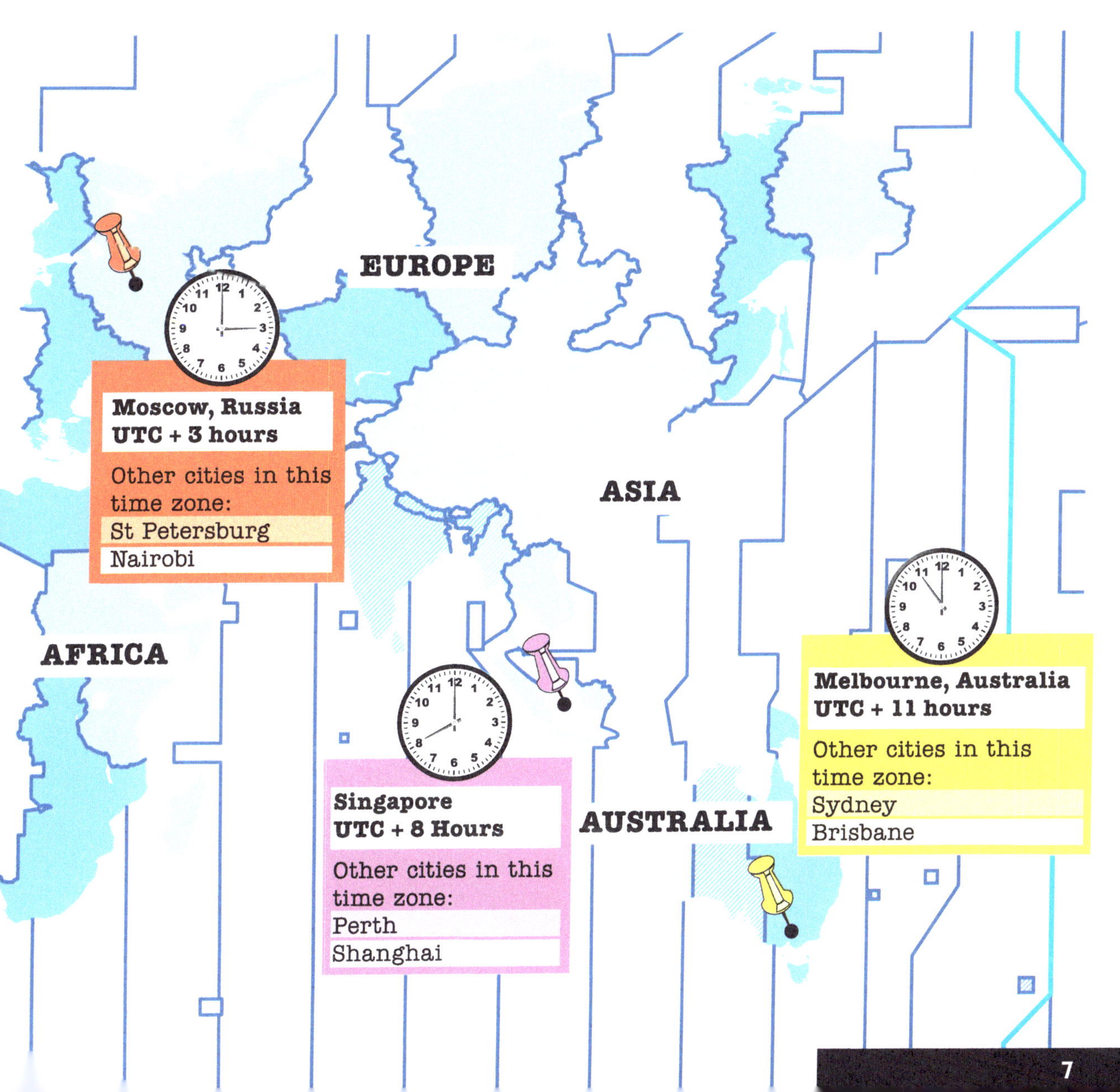

2 Hello from Vancouver

Emily's Email from Vancouver, Canada

"Hello my name is Emily. I live in Vancouver. In my time zone it is 4.00 pm. My city is the best place in the world to live in. Let me tell you why."

Time: 4.00 pm in Vancouver

= 12.00 am in London
= 3.00 am in Moscow
= 8.00 am in Singapore
= 11.00 am in Melbourne due to daylight savings

Date: 30 November
Day: Sunday
Season: autumn or "fall"

collecting autumn leaves

Weather: It is 4.00 pm on Sunday afternoon. It is only one degree Celsius. Our top temperature today was only six degrees Celsius. We had snow in November. This is unusual. People say that our climate is changing.

In Vancouver it's 4 o'clock on Sunday afternoon.

Climate: Our climate is "oceanic". Tomorrow we will have a low temperature of one degree Celsius and a high temperature of seven degrees Celsius. We don't get much snow but we do get a lot of rain!

Score out of 10 = ☐

Air Quality: Vancouver has about 600 000 people. We're the smallest city in this time-zone competition but the air pollution is getting worse. The number of cars is growing faster than the population! When the wind blows the pollution in towards the city, the mountains trap the pollution and stop it from moving away from the city.

Score out of 10 = ☐

Social Studies

Thanksgiving in Canada

One national holiday in Canada is Thanksgiving. The Canadian people celebrate Thanksgiving on the second Monday in October.

They share lunch or dinner with family and friends. Most people have a traditional meal of roast turkey, vegetables and pumpkin pie.

the Canadian flag

Environment: Vancouver is on the west coast of Canada. In October – our autumn or fall – the leaves on thousands of maple trees turn orange, deep red, pink and golden yellow. Most maple trees have lost their leaves now.

The North Shore Mountains tower above the city. People go snowshoeing, snowboarding, mountain biking, hiking and abseiling in these mountains.

Score out of 10 = ☐

skiing at Grouse Mountain

Highlights: The highlight tomorrow is a school trip to Grouse Mountain. It will be fun!

On Grouse Mountain, we will ski, go mountain biking and hiking, snowboard and ice-skate.

The highlight of the year is our two-month holiday in the summer – July and August!

Score out of 10 = ☐

Grouse Mountain

At Grouse Mountain you can learn about:

- endangered wildlife
- the traditional way of life for the first people of Canada
- trees, plants and animals.

Emily's Conclusion: Despite the rain and the pollution, Vancouver is a beautiful city. There are great mountains and a lot to do in summer and winter. I wouldn't want to live anywhere else in the world.

"Goodbye from Vancouver, Emily."

Total Score for Vancouver = ☐ /50

Hello from London

Nick's Email from London, United Kingdom

"**Hello** my name is Nick. I live in London. In my time zone it is 12.00 am. My city is the best place in the world to live in. Let me tell you why."

Time: **12.00 am in London**
= 3.00 am in Moscow
= 8.00 am in Singapore
= 11.00 am in Melbourne due to daylight savings
= 4.00 pm in Vancouver

Date: 1 December
Day: Monday
Season: winter

Weather: This morning is a chilly three degrees Celsius. Our top temperature today will be nine degrees Celsius. There will be light rain today. We get regular, steady rain throughout the year. Heavy downpours are rare.

Score out of 10 = ☐

Climate: Our climate is "oceanic", like Vancouver and Melbourne. We have colder winters than Melbourne, but our summers are not as hot.

Score out of 10 = ☐

In London it's 12 o'clock on Monday morning.

Air Quality: London can have bad air pollution in December. The pollution comes from cars, factories, dust from building works and other things. There is very little wind to blow pollution away. It can hang around in the foggy, winter air.

Score out of 10 = ☐

Environment: Our city is on the Thames river. The Thames is a tidal river. In the past, high tides flooded parts of London. Now we have a huge barrier that can close the river off if the tides are too high.

Score out of 10 = ☐

the London Eye

Technology

What's the London Eye?

The London Eye is a giant Ferris wheel, 135 metres high. It was opened on the last day of the millennium, 31 December 1999. There are 32 glass capsules that can each hold 25 people. People can see landmarks such as the Tower of London and the famous clock, Big Ben.

a London bus and Big Ben

Highlights: Seeing my friends is a highlight. We go to a small, inner-city primary school. London's buildings are built very close together so we don't have much playground space at school.

After school, my parents are taking my friends and I to the London Eye – a massive Ferris wheel!

Soon, we will have two weeks holiday for Christmas and New Year. Our new school term will start at the beginning of January.

Score out of 10 = ☐

Nick's Conclusion: Living in London is great. I like riding on the buses and going to all of the attractions. There's always something to do.

"Goodbye from London, Nick."

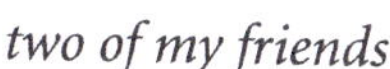

two of my friends

Total Score for London = ☐ /50

the flag of the United Kingdom

Hello from Moscow

Alena's Email from Moscow, Russia

"**Hello** my name is Alena. I live in Moscow. In my time zone it is 3.00 am. My city is the best place in the world to live in. Let me tell you why."

Time: **3.00 am in Moscow**
= 8.00 am in Singapore
= 11.00 am in Melbourne due to daylight savings
= 4.00 pm in Vancouver
= 12.00 am in London

Date: 1 December
Day: Monday
Season: winter (Moscow has two main seasons – six months of winter and six months of summer)

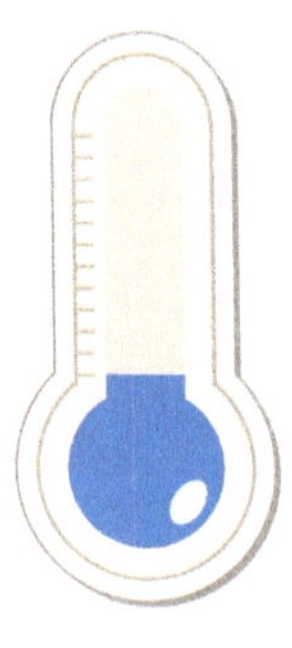

dressed for minus ten degrees Celsius

Weather: Today it snowed again. The temperature this morning was minus ten degrees Celsius. It may not get higher than minus three degrees Celsius today. It's freezing but we're used to it!

Score out of 10 = ☐

In Moscow it's 3 o'clock on Monday morning.

Climate: Our climate is "humid continental". We have warm, humid summers but long, freezing winters! We have snow from about November which may not melt until March.

Score out of 10 = ☐

Air Quality: Moscow has very bad air pollution. It comes mainly from power stations burning coal, millions of cars, and big industries.

Many children get asthma. Our government is trying to improve air quality but it may take many years.

Score out of 10 = ☐

Social Studies

Winter at Gorky Park

In winter, Moscow's Gorky Park is great fun. The park's footpaths are flooded and then frozen so children can ice-skate around the play areas.

In February, families can create ice sculptures, too.

the Russian flag

Environment: Moscow is far from the sea. Mountains stop warm air coming up from hotter countries in the south. But mountains do not stop cold weather coming down from the freezing Arctic region.

This means that Moscow and other parts of Russia can have snow for six months of the year!

Score out of 10 = ☐

Highlights: I'm in third grade in an elementary school. My friends have been in my class for the last three years. I'm glad we'll be in the same class next year as well. We have the same teacher right through school. Next year will be our last year in elementary school.

The best part of the year is the three-month summer holiday. It is in June, July and August.

Score out of 10 = ☐

Alena's Conclusion: If you like snow, then Moscow is a great place to live. It's fun ice-skating with my family and friends. I love it!

"Goodbye from Moscow, Alena."

Total Score for Moscow = ☐ **/50**

5 Hello from Singapore

Matt's Email from Singapore, Republic of Singapore

"**Hello** my name is Matt. I live in Singapore. In my time zone it is 8.00 am. My city is the best place in the world to live in. Let me tell you why."

Time: **8.00 am in Singapore**
= 11.00 am in Melbourne due to daylight savings
= 4.00 pm in Vancouver
= 12.00 am in London
= 3.00 am in Moscow

Date: 1 December
Day: Monday
Season: There are two types of tropical seasons – the north-east monsoon season (November to March) and the south-west monsoon season (May to September)

Weather: This morning is humid and warm. It is 23 degrees Celsius. Our top temperature today will be 31 degrees Celsius.

From December to early March we have our first north-east monsoon. Very heavy rain falls. It's great weather for the gardens, and to fill our water catchments.

Score out of 10 = ☐

In Singapore it's 8 o'clock on Monday morning.

Climate: Our climate is "tropical wet". It is hot and humid all year. Heavy rains fall as tropical storms throughout the year. There are no frosts. It's a great place to grow plants. They can grow all year round.

Score out of 10 = ☐

Air Quality: Our city has almost five million people. Strong winds in December keep our air clean.

Score out of 10 = ☐

Environment: Singapore is an island city, which lies close to the equator. Almost half of our small island is forests or open, green areas. The other half is for homes and businesses.

A small area is used for growing food. Most of our food is imported from other countries.

Score out of 10 = ☐

Technology

Domestic Water Supply

About half of Singapore's water comes from rain collected in reservoirs. In 2005, Asia's largest desalination plant was opened in Singapore.

the flag of Singapore

holiday time

my family enjoys the garden

Highlights: We're on "long holidays" now. They started at the end of November, and we don't go back to school until January.

My friends and I do lots of holiday activities, but my favourite is on Friday nights. We go to a four-hour pizza party and movie at a kids' gym. My parents drive us there at 5.00 pm and pick us up at 9.00 pm.

Score out of 10 = ☐

Matt's Conclusion: Singapore is a busy city but the beautiful gardens and parks mean you can get away from the city for some fun. I like the hot weather because I love swimming. It's my favourite thing about Singapore.

"Goodbye from Singapore, Matt."

Total Score for Singapore = ☐ /50

6 Hello from Melbourne

Jackson's Email from Melbourne, Australia

"Hello my name is Jackson. I live in Melbourne. In my time zone it is 8.00 am. My city is the best place in the world to live in. Let me tell you why."

Time: **11.00 am in Melbourne**
due to daylight savings
= 4.00 pm in Vancouver
= 12.00 am in London
= 3.00 am in Moscow
= 8.00 am in Singapore

Date: 1 December
Day: Monday
Season: first day of summer

Weather: This morning the weather was cool. The temperature was ten degrees Celsius. Our top temperature today will be a warm 20 degrees Celsius. That's great weather for our first day of summer.

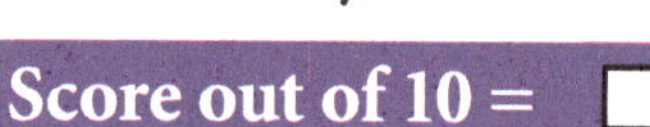

my friends love the beach in summer

In Melbourne it's 11 o'clock on Monday morning.

Climate: Our climate is "oceanic". But on some days, the wind changes. Northerly winds can be very hot. Southerly winds can be very cold!

Score out of 10 = ☐

Environment: We haven't had much rain for years. This means that we don't have enough water in our reservoirs. In Melbourne, people have to save water wherever they can.

At home, we have four-minute showers. We collect our shower water in a bucket to water our gardens.

The grass in the parks and gardens is still green. Recycled water is used to keep it alive. But many people's gardens have brown patches of grass. We need more rain, urgently!

Score out of 10 = ☐

Melbourne, AUSTRALIA

History

Hot, Northerly Winds

On 7 February 2009, there were strong northerly winds and the highest recorded temperatures in Victoria. Melbourne reached almost 46 degrees Celsius. Raging bushfires started and burnt hundreds of homes and thousands of trees in country areas. Many people and animals lost their lives.

the flag of Australia

Air Quality: Our city has over four million people. Cars and industries cause air pollution. Melbourne is on the south coast of Australia, so sea breezes blow away the pollution on most days. Autumn days without wind can be smoggy.

Score out of 10 = ☐

Highlights: There is no school today. It is a pupil-free day. Our teachers go to school but we don't! I'm going to the beach with my family.

swimming at the beach

Some Melbourne suburbs are close to great beaches around the bay. We surf, swim and build sandcastles at the beach. We love exploring the rock pools. Our family will cook food on a barbecue at the beach.

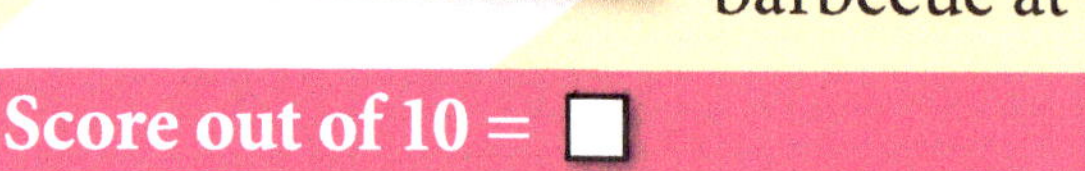

Score out of 10 = ☐

Jackson's Conclusion: At times Melbourne may not get enough rain but that means we get lots of sunshine. I'd much rather be outdoors than stuck inside all the time!

"Goodbye from Melbourne, Jackson."

Total Score for Melbourne = ☐ /50

7 And the Winner Is ...

Grouse Mountain, Vancouver, Canada

Make Your Own Score Chart

Create a score chart similar to the one on this page. Write the total scores for each city on your chart.
And the winner is ...?

A Scoring Chart Example

Total Score for Vancouver = ☐

Parliament House and Big Ben, London, the United Kingdom

Red Square, Moscow, Russia

the Yarra River, Melbourne, Australia

the city skyline, Singapore

Index

Glossary

Celsius	A measurement of temperature where 0°C is freezing point and 100°C is boiling point
desalination plant	A place where technology is used to take salt out of sea water so it becomes drinkable
equator	An imaginary line around the middle of Earth, dividing it into the Northern and Southern Hemispheres
hemispheres	The northern and southern halves of a sphere, in this case Earth, divided by the equator
humid	Air containing high amounts of water vapour, which makes it feel warm and moist
oceanic	To do with the ocean; an oceanic climate usually has temperatures that are not too hot in summer and not too cold in winter
reservoir	A large lake, dam or tank used as a water supply for a town or city
universal	Applies to everyone or everything